A WISHING–CHAIR
ADVENTURE

THE WITCH'S
LOST CAT

For Louisa and Isabella
A. P.

EGMONT
We bring stories to life

Cover and interior illustrations by Alex Paterson

Text first published in Great Britain as chapters 4-9
of *The Adventures of the Wishing-Chair*, 1937 by Newnes
Published as *The Witch's Lost Cat: A Wishing-Chair Adventure*, 2019
by Egmont UK Limited
The Yellow Building, 1 Nicholas Road, London W11 4AN

Enid Blyton ®, The Magic Faraway Tree ®
and Enid Blyton's signature are registered trade marks of
Hodder & Stoughton Limited
Text © 1937 Hodder & Stoughton Limited
Illustrations © 2019 Hodder & Stoughton Limited

ISBN 978 1 4052 9269 6

www.egmont.co.uk

A CIP catalogue record for this title is available from the British Library

Printed in Malaysia

70220/001

Enid Blyton

A WISHING-CHAIR
ADVENTURE

THE WITCH'S
LOST CAT

EGMONT

THE WISHING-CHAIR what magical adventure will it take the children on next?

The playroom at the bottom of the garden is where nearly all the wishing-chair's adventures begin . . .

PETER

MOLLIE

BINKY is the most helpful pixie you ever did meet

CHAPTER ONE
THE HO-HO WIZARD

One day when Peter and Mollie ran down to see Binky the pixie in their playroom, they found him reading a letter and groaning loudly.

'What's the matter, Binky?' said the children, in **surprise**. 'Oh, I've had a letter from my cousin, Gobo,' said Binky. 'Gobo says that my village is very unhappy because a wizard has come to live there, called Ho-Ho. He is a horrid fellow, and walks about saying, "Ho, ho!" all the time, catching the little pixies to help him in his magic, and putting all kinds of **spells** on any one that goes against him. I feel very unhappy.'

'Oh, Binky, we're so sorry!' said the children at once. 'Can't we help?'

'I don't think so,' said Binky sadly. 'But I would **very much** like to go off in the wishing-chair to my village, next time it grows wings, if you don't mind.'

'Of course!' said the children.

Then Mollie cried out in delight, and pointed to the magic chair. 'Look! It's growing wings now! **How lovely!** It must have heard what we said.'

'We'll all go,' said Peter, feeling excited to think that yet another adventure had begun.

'Oh, no,' said Binky at once. 'I'd better go alone. This wizard is a **horrid** one. He might quite well catch you, as you are clever children, and then think how dreadful I would feel!'

'I don't care!' said Peter. 'We're coming!'

He and Mollie went to the chair and sat firmly down in it. Binky went to it and sat down too, squeezing in between the two. 'You are such **nice children!**' he said happily.

The chair creaked, and before it could fly off, the pixie cried out loudly, '**Go to the village of Apple-pie!**'

It flew slowly out of the door, flapping its rose-red wings. The children were used to flying off in the magic chair now, but they were just as excited as ever. The village of Apple-pie! How **magic** it sounded!

It didn't take them very long to get there. The chair put them down in the middle of the village street, and was at once surrounded by an **excited crowd** of pixies, who shook hands with Binky and asked him a hundred questions.

He talked at the top of his voice, explained who the children were, and why he had come. Then suddenly there was a **great silence**, and every one turned pale. The **Ho-ho Wizard** was coming down the street!

He was a little fellow, with a long flowing cloak that swirled out as he walked and showed its bright golden lining. On his head he wore a round tight cap set with silver bells that tinkled loudly. He wore three pairs of glasses on his long nose, and a beard that hung in three pieces down to his waist. He really was a queer-looking fellow.

'Ho, ho!' he said, as he came near the pixies. 'What have we here? Visitors? And, bless us all, this is a wishing-chair, **as sure as dogs have tails!** Well, well, well!'

Nobody said anything at all. The wizard

prodded the chair with a long stick and then turned to the children.

'Ho, ho!' he said, blinking at them through his pairs of glasses. '**Ho, ho!** So you have a magic chair. Pray come to have a cup of cocoa with me this morning, and I will buy your chair from you.'

'But we don't want to sell it,' began Peter at once. The wizard turned round on him, and from his eyes there came what looked like real **sparks**. He was very angry.

'How dare you refuse me anything!' he cried. 'I will turn you into a –'

'We will come in half an hour,' stammered Binky, pushing Peter behind him. 'This boy did not understand how important you are, **Sir Wizard**.'

'Brrrrrrrrr!' said the wizard, and stalked off, his cloak flying out behind him.

12

CHAPTER TWO
GOBO'S COTTAGE

'*Now* what are we to do?' said Peter, in dismay. 'Can't we get into the chair and **fly off**, Binky. Do let's!'

'No, no, don't!' cried all the pixies at once. 'If you do, Ho-ho will punish the whole village, and that will be terrible. Stay here and help us.'

'Come to my cousin Gobo's cottage and let us think,' said Binky. So the two children went with him and Gobo, who was really very like Binky, to a **little crooked cottage** at the end of the village.

It was beautifully clean and neat, and the children sat down to eat **coconut cakes** and drink lemonade. Everyone was rather quiet. Then Peter's eyes began to twinkle, and he leaned over to Gobo.

'I say, Gobo, have you by any chance got a spell to put people to sleep?' he asked.

'Of course!' said Gobo, puzzled. 'Why?'

'Well, I have a fine plan,' said Peter. 'What about putting old Ho-ho to sleep?'

'What's the use of that?' said Binky and Gobo.

'Well – when he's asleep, we'll pop him into the magic chair, take him off somewhere and leave him, and then go back home ourselves!' said Peter. 'That would get rid of him for you, wouldn't it?'

'My goodness! **That's an idea!**' cried

Binky, jumping up from his seat in excitement. 'Gobo! If only we could do it! Listen! Where's the **sleepy-spell?**'

'Here,' said Gobo, opening a drawer and taking out a tiny yellow thing like a mustard seed.

'Well, Peter has a **bag of chocolates**,' said Binky, 'and he could put the sleepy-spell into one of them and give it to Ho-ho.'

'But how do we know he'd take the right chocolate?' asked Mollie.

'We'll empty out all of them except one,' answered Binky, 'and that one Peter shall carry in the bag in his hand, and he must carry it as though it was something **very precious** indeed, and Ho-ho is sure to ask him what it is, and if Peter says it is a very special chocolate that he is not going to part with, or something like that, the old wizard is sure to be greedy enough to take it from him and eat it. Then he will fall asleep, and we'll take him off in the chair to **old Dame Tap-Tap**, who will be so pleased to have him! He once tried to turn her into a ladybird, so I don't think she will let him go in a hurry!'

'Good idea!' cried everyone, and Gobo danced round the room so excitedly that he fell over the coal scuttle and sent the fire-irons clanking to the floor. That made them all laugh, and they felt **so excited** that they could hardly empty out Peter's bag of chocolates on the table and choose one for the sleepy-spell.

They chose a chocolate with a violet on top
because it looked **so grand**. Peter made a
little hole in it and popped in the spell. Then
he left the rest of the chocolates with Gobo,
who said he would enjoy them very much, put
the violet one into the bag, and went off to get
the wishing-chair with the others.

It was still standing in the market-place, its
red wings hanging down, for it was tired.
Binky and Peter thought they might as well

carry it to Ho-ho's cottage, which was only in the next street; so **off they went**, taking it on their shoulders.

Ho-ho was waiting for them, his wily face watching from a **window**. He opened the door, and they all went in with the chair.

'I see you have brought me the chair,' said Ho-ho. 'Very sensible of you! Now sit down and have a **cup of cocoa**.'

He poured out some very thin cocoa for them, made without any milk, and looked at them all sharply. He at once saw that Peter was holding something very carefully in his hand, which he did not even put down when he was drinking his cocoa.

'What have you got in your hand?' he asked.

'Something I want to keep!' said Peter at once.

'Show me,' said the wizard eagerly.

'No,' said Peter.

'**Show me!**' ordered the wizard angrily.

Peter pretended to be frightened, and at once put the paper bag on the table. The wizard took it and opened it. He took out the chocolate.

'Ho, ho! The finest chocolate I ever saw!' he said, and **licked it** to see what it tasted like.

'Don't eat it, oh, don't eat it!' cried Peter at once, pretending to be most upset. 'It's mine!'

'Well, now it's mine!' said the wizard, and he popped it into his mouth and chewed it up. And no sooner had he swallowed it than his head began to nod, his eyes closed, and he snored like **twenty pigs** grunting!

'The spell has worked, the spell has worked!' cried Peter, jumping about in excitement.

25

'Now, Peter, there's no time to jump and yell,' said Binky hurriedly. 'The spell may stop at any time, and we **don't** want to wake up the wizard till we've got him to Dame Tap-Tap's. Help me to put him into the chair.'

Between them they dumped the sleeping wizard into the chair. Then Mollie sat on one arm, Peter sat on the other, and Binky sat right on the top of the back. 'To Dame Tap-Tap!' he cried. At once the wishing-chair flapped its idle wings, flew out of the door, and up into the air, cheered by all the **pixies** in the village. What a thrill that was!

In about five minutes the chair flew downwards again to a small cottage set right on the top of a **windy** hill. It was Dame Tap-Tap's home. The chair flew down to her front door, outside which there was a wooden bench. The three of them pulled the **snoring** wizard out of the chair and put him on the bench.

Then Binky took hold of the knocker and banged it hard, four times. 'Rat-tat-tat-tat!'

He yelled at the top of his voice: 'Dame
Tap-Tap! Here's a present for you!'

Then he and the children bundled into the wishing-chair again, and off they flew into the air, leaning over to see the old dame crying out in astonishment and **delight** when she opened the door and found the wizard Ho-ho sleeping outside!

'What a shock for him when he wakes up!' said Binky, with a grin. 'Well, children, many, many thanks for your help. You've saved **Apple-pie village** from a very nasty fellow. It will be nice to think of him dusting Dame Tap-Tap's kitchen, and getting water for her from the well! I guess she'll make him work hard!'

'Ho, ho!' roared the children, as the chair flew down to their playroom. 'Perhaps the wizard won't say **"ho, ho"** quite so much to Dame Tap-Tap!'

'No! He might get a spanking if he did,' grinned Binky. 'Well, here we are! See you tomorrow, children!'

CHAPTER THREE
THE LOST CAT

One morning it was very wet, and Mollie, Peter, and Binky were playing a very noisy game of **snap** in the playroom together. Whiskers, the cat, had come with them and had curled herself up on a cushion in the wishing-chair, where she had gone fast asleep.

'Snap! Snap! SNAP!' yelled the children – and were so interested in their game that they didn't hear a little **flapping** sound. The wishing-chair had grown its wings and was flapping them gently to and fro. Before any one noticed the chair rose silently into the air and flew out of the open door – taking the puss-cat with it, still fast asleep!

'Snap!' yelled Binky, and took the last pile of cards in glee. 'I've won!'

'Good,' said Peter. He looked round the playroom to see what game to play next – and then he looked rather **surprised** and scared.

'I say!' he said. 'Where's the chair gone?'

Binky and Mollie looked round too. Mollie went pale. 'It's gone!' she said.

'It was here when we began our game,' said Binky. 'It must have slipped out without us noticing. I sort of remember feeling a little draught. It must have been its wings flapping.'

'Whiskers has gone too!' said Mollie, in alarm. 'She was asleep on the cushion. Oh, Binky – will she come back?'

'Depends where she has gone to,' said Binky. 'She's a **black cat**, you know – and if a witch should see her she might take her to help in her spells. Black cats are clever with spells.'

Mollie began to cry. She was very fond of

Whiskers. 'Oh, why did we let Whiskers go to sleep on that chair?' she wept.

'Well, it's no good crying,' said Binky, patting Mollie's shoulder. 'We must just **wait and see**. Perhaps old Whiskers will come back still fast asleep when the chair returns!'

They waited for an hour or two with the door wide open – but no wishing-chair came back. The two children left Binky and went to their dinner. They **hunted** about the house just in case Whiskers should have got off the chair cushion and wandered home – but no one had seen her.

After dinner they ran down the garden to
their playroom again. Binky was there, looking
gloomy.

'The chair hasn't come back,' he said.

But, just as he spoke, Peter gave a shout and pointed up into the sky. There was the chair, flapping its way back, all its red wings **twinkling** up and down.

'Look! There's the chair! Oh, I do hope Whiskers is on her cushion. Suppose she has fallen out!'

The chair flapped its way downwards, and flew in at the open door. It came to rest in its usual place and gave a sigh and a creak. The children **rushed** to it.

There was no cat there! The cushion was still in its place, with a dent in the middle where Whiskers had lain – but that was all!

CHAPTER FOUR
LOOMA, LOOMA, LOOMA, LOO

The three stared at one another in dismay.

'Whiskers has been caught by a witch,' said Binky. 'There's no doubt about it. Look at this!' He picked up a **tiny silver star** that lay on the seat of the chair. 'This little star has fallen off a witch's embroidered cloak.'

'Poor Whiskers!' wept Mollie. 'I do want her back. Oh, Binky, what shall we do?'

'Well, we'd better find out first where she's gone,' said Binky. 'Then, the next time the chair grows its wings we'll go and **rescue** her.'

'How can we find out where she's gone?'

asked Mollie, drying her eyes.

'I'll have to work a spell to find that out,' said Binky. 'I'll have to get a few pixies in to help me. Go and sit down on the couch, Mollie and Peter, and don't speak a word until I've finished. The pixies won't help me if you interfere. They are very shy just about here.'

Mollie and Peter did as they were told. They sat down on the couch feeling rather excited. Binky went to the open door and clapped his hands softly three times, then **loudly** seven times. He whistled like a blackbird, and then called a magic word that sounded like 'Looma, looma, looma, loo'. In a minute or two four little pixies, a bit smaller than Binky, who was himself a pixie, came **running** in at the door. They stopped when they saw the two children, but Binky said they were his friends.

'They won't interfere,' he said. 'I want to do a spell to find out where this wishing-chair has just been to. Will you help me?'

The pixies **twittered** like swallows and nodded their heads. Binky sat down in the wishing-chair, holding in his hands a mirror that he had borrowed from Mollie. The four little pixies joined hands and **danced round**

the chair, first one way and then another, chanting a magic song that got higher and higher and **quicker and quicker** as they danced round in time to their singing.

Binky looked intently into the mirror, and the children watched, wondering what he would see there.

Suddenly the four dancing pixies stopped their singing and fell to the floor, panting and crying, 'Now look and tell what you see, Binky!'

Binky stared into the mirror and then gave a shout.

'I see her! It's the **witch Kirri-Kirri!** She has got Whiskers. Here she is, cooking her dinner for her!'

The two children sprang up from the couch and hurried to look into the mirror that Binky held. To their **great amazement**, instead of seeing their own faces, they saw a picture of Whiskers, their cat, stirring a soup-pot on a big stove – and behind her was an old witch, clad in a long, black cloak embroidered with silver stars and moons!

'See her!' said Binky, pointing. 'That's the witch Kirri-Kirri. I know where she lives. We'll go and **rescue Whiskers** this very night – even if we have to go on foot!'

The four little pixies twittered goodbye and ran out. The picture in the mirror faded away. The children and the pixie looked at one another.

'What a marvellous spell!' said Mollie. 'Oh, I did enjoy that, Binky! Shall we really go and fetch Whiskers tonight?'

'Yes,' said Binky. 'Come here at **midnight**, ready dressed. If the chair has grown its wings, we'll go in it – if not, we'll take the underground train to the witch's house.'

'Ooh!' said Mollie. 'What an adventure!'

CHAPTER FIVE
THE WITCH KIRRI-KIRRI

The children dressed themselves again after

they had been to bed and slept. Mollie had a little alarm clock and she set it for a quarter to twelve, so they awoke in good time for their **adventure**.

Binky was waiting for them.

'We can't go in the wishing-chair,' he said. 'It hasn't grown its wings again. I think it's asleep, because it gave a **tiny snore** just now!'

'How funny!' said Mollie. 'Oh, Binky – I do feel excited!'

'Come on,' said the pixie. 'There's no time to lose if we want to catch the underground train.'

He led the children to a big tree at the bottom of the garden. He **twisted** a piece of the bark and a door slid open. There was a narrow stairway in the tree going downwards. Mollie and Peter were so surprised to see it.

'Go down the stairs,' Binky said to them. 'I'll just shut the door behind us.'

They climbed down and came to a small passage. Binky joined them and they went along it until they came to a big turnstile, where a solemn **grey rabbit** sat holding a bundle of tickets.

'We want tickets for Witch Kirri-Kirri's,' said Binky. The rabbit gave them three yellow tickets and let them through the turnstile. There was a little platform beyond with a railway line running by it. Almost at once a train appeared out of the darkness. Its lamps **gleamed** like two eyes.

There were no carriages – just open trucks with cushions in. The train was very crowded, and the children and Binky found it difficult to get seats.

Gnomes, brownies, rabbits, moles, elves, and hedgehogs sat in the trucks, **chattering** and laughing. The two hedgehogs had a truck to themselves for they were **so prickly** that no one wanted to sit by them.

The train set off with much clattering. It
stopped at station after station, and at last came
to one labelled **'Kirri-Kirri Station'**.

Binky and the children got out.

'Kirri-Kirri is such a rich and powerful
witch that she has a station of her own,'

explained Binky. 'Now listen – this is my plan, children. It's no use us asking the witch for Whiskers, our cat – she just won't let us have her. And it's no use trying to get her by magic, because the witch's magic is much **stronger** than mine. We must get her by a trick.'

'What trick?' asked the children.

'We'll creep into her little garden,' said Binky, 'and we'll make scrapey noises on the wall, like mice. We'll squeak like mice too – and the witch will hear us and send Whiskers out to catch the mice. Then we'll get her, run back to the station, and catch the next train home!'

'What a **fine plan**!' said Peter. 'It's so simple too! It can't go wrong!'

'Sh!' said Binky, pointing to a large house in the distance. 'That's Kirri-Kirri's house.'

They had left the station behind and

had come up into the open air again. The **moonlight** was bright enough to show them the road, and they could see everything very clearly indeed.

They slipped inside the witch's wicket-gate. 'You go to that end of the house and I'll go to the other,' said Binky. So Peter and Mollie crept to one end and began to scratch against the wall with bits of stick, whilst Binky did the same the other end. Then they **squeaked** as high as they could, exactly like mice.

They heard a window being thrown up, and saw the witch's head outlined against the lamplight.

'**Mice again!**' she grumbled. 'Hi, Whiskers, come here! Catch them, catch them!' Whiskers jumped down into the garden. The witch slammed down the window and drew the blind. Mollie made a dash for the **big black cat** and lifted her into her arms. Whiskers purred nineteen to the dozen and rubbed her soft head against Mollie's hand. Binky and Peter came up in delight.

'The plan worked beautifully!' said Peter. 'Come on – let's go to the station!'

And then a most unfortunate thing happened! Peter fell over a bush and came down with a loud **clatter** on the path! At once the window flew up again and Kirri-Kirri looked out. She shouted a very magic word and slammed the window down again.

'Oh dear, oh dear, **oh dear!**' groaned Binky at once. 'What's the matter?' asked Mollie, scared.

'She's put a spell round the garden!' said the pixie. 'We can't get out! She'll find us here in the morning!'

'Can't get out!' said Peter, going to the gate. '**What nonsense!** I'm going, anyway!'

But although he opened the gate he couldn't walk out. It was as if there was an invisible wall

all round the garden! The children couldn't get out anywhere. They forced their way through the hedge – but still the invisible wall seemed to be just beyond, and there was no way of getting out at all!

'Whatever shall we do?' asked Mollie.

'We can't do anything,' said Binky gloomily. 'Peter was an awful silly to go and fall over like that, just when we had done everything so well.'

'I'm terribly sorry,' said poor Peter. 'I do wish I hadn't. I didn't mean to.'

'Well, we'd better go and sit down in the porch,' said Binky, who was shivering. 'It's **warmer** there.'

They sat huddled together in the porch and Mollie took Whiskers on her knee, saying she would make a nice hot-water bottle.

They were nodding off to sleep, for they were all very tired, when Whiskers **suddenly** began to snarl and spit. The children and Binky woke up in a fright. They saw something flying round the garden, like a big black bird! Mollie stared – and then she leapt up and whispered as loudly as she dared – 'It isn't a bird! It's the dear old wishing-chair! It's come to find us!'

Binky gave a **chuckle** of delight. He ran to the chair and took hold of it.

'Come on!' he said to the others. 'The only way out of this bewitched garden is by flying **up and up**. We can't get out any other way! The wishing-chair is just what we want!' They all got into the chair. Whiskers was on Mollie's knee. The chair flapped its wings, rose up into the air and flew almost to the clouds!

'What will old Kirri-Kirri say in the morning when she finds no one in her garden, not even Whiskers!' giggled Binky. 'She'll think she's been **dreaming**! I wish I could see her face!'

The chair flew to the playroom. The children said **goodnight** to Binky, and, with Whiskers in her arms, Mollie ran with Peter up the path to their house. They were soon in bed and **asleep**. As for Whiskers, you may be sure she never went to sleep in the wishing-chair again!

The FARAWAY TREE Adventures

Collect all the magical FARAWAY TREE Adventures – packed full of exciting new colour illustrations!